First published in the United States
of America in 1989 by The Mallard Press

Mallard Press and its accompanying design
and logo are trademarks of BDD Promotional
Book Company, Inc.

Produced by
Twin Books
15 Sherwood Place
Greenwich, CT 06830

ISBN 0-792-45236-4

Printed in Hong Kong

SWEET DUCK
OF YOUTH

Twin Books

MALLARD
PRESS

Huey, Dewey and Louie, Launchpad McQuack and Mrs. Beakley sang "Happy Birthday" to Scrooge McDuck as he opened his present. When he saw it, he almost cried. It was a rocking chair. "It's the perfect gift," said Mrs. Beakley happily.

"Am I really that old?" thought Scrooge, suddenly tired. "Why, it seems like only yesterday I made me first million. Oh, if only I could go back...if only I could find the Fountain of Youth!"

That idea sent him rushing to his library. A moment later the others found him smiling down at a book in his hands.

"Pack your bags, lads. We're goin' to Florida!" said Scrooge.

"Going to Florida?" repeated Launchpad. "To do what?"

"To find the Fountain of Youth," said Scrooge.

"Isn't that just a legend, Uncle Scrooge?" asked Huey.

"Not according to this book," said Scrooge. "Ponce de Leon found it somewhere in Florida. Come on! We're leaving right away!"

Hours later, the helicopter was flying over the Florida Everglades.

A man dressed like an old Spanish soldier watched the helicopter overhead. He aimed his crossbow at the helicopter and let the arrow fly.

"We've lost control!" yelled Launchpad. "Get ready for an emergency landing!"

The helicopter landed in a swamp.

"Everyone out!" cried Scrooge. "We'll meet on dry land."

Scrooge's nephews got out first and grabbed a log that floated by. Scrooge ended up at the other side of a hill, separated from everyone else.

Unable to find Launchpad or his nephews, Scrooge set up a shelter where he could spend the night. He lit a fire to keep warm, and hoped that Launchpad and the boys would see the fire and join him. Someone else joined him, instead.

Scrooge let out a yell. A Spanish conqueror was coming towards him, and an ax was in his hand.

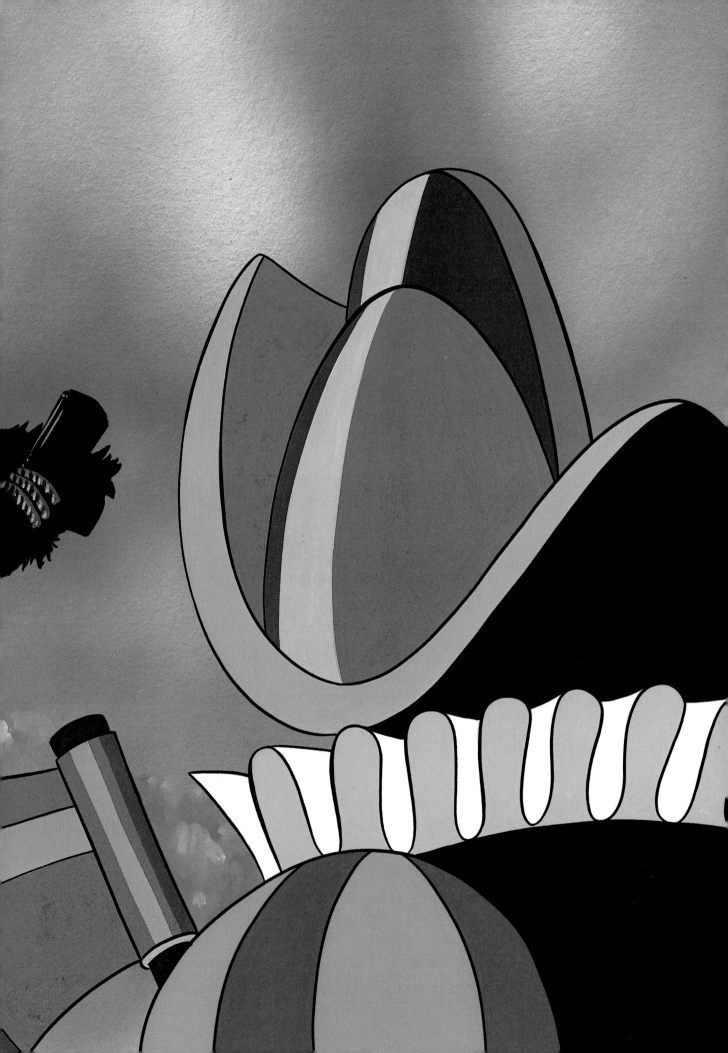

Scrooge had fainted. When he woke up, he found himself in a net hanging from the ceiling of a shack. He saw Launchpad hanging right next to him. The Spanish soldier stood guard.

Meanwhile, Huey, Dewey and Louie had found the shack. Watching for danger, they tiptoed up to it and peeked through the window.

"Look, Unca Scrooge and Launchpad are prisoners!" said Huey.

"There's a guy dressed like an old Spanish soldier. Why would he be dressed that way?" said Dewey.

"Boy, is he old!" said Louie.

"Why are you holding us prisoner?" asked Scrooge.

"You've come to steal my secret," answered the old man.

"Your secret? We didn't even know you lived here."

"Don't lie! You want to steal the map to the Fountain of Youth."

"You have the map?" asked Scrooge, doubtfully. "No, that's impossible. If you had it, you wouldn't be so old."

When the old man left the house, Scrooge's nephews freed the prisoners.

The stranger returned, no longer wearing his armor. He sighed. "I see you are not alone. I might as well tell you my story.

"I came here many years ago looking for the Fountain of Youth. I found this old suit of armor and, inside the helmet, was a map that showed exactly where the fountain was."

"Well, where is it?" Scrooge wanted to know.

"At the old mission. But I warn you, the fountain is dry."

"We'll go there in the morning," Scrooge decided.

At sunrise, the group stood before the ruins of the Spanish mission.

The fountain had been well cared for, but no water had poured through it in years. Everyone knew how disappointed Scrooge was, and they all stood around the fountain in silence.

Suddenly, the bricks underneath their feet gave way, and they dropped down into a river that flowed through an underground cave.

It seemed as if the river carried them for hours until, finally, they came to a stop in a large cave, where the water was calm.

"Look!" shouted Launchpad, pointing to the cave walls.

Giant figures were carved into the rock, and water squirted from their mouths. It was the Fountain of Youth.

Scrooge looked into the waters, and screamed with surprise. The Scrooge who looked back at him was 40 years younger!

"So, this is the secret of the fountain!" said the old man, looking into the water himself. "The water doesn't make you younger, it only shows you what you looked like when you were younger."

"I was really good-lookin', wasn't I?" said Scrooge. "But I still like meself the way I am. I think I'm more interestin'."

On their way back to civilization, everyone felt worn out. Everyone, that is, except Scrooge, who acted 40 years younger!

It was time to return to Duckburg. The old man went to the airport with them to say goodbye.

"I hope you'll come again," he said, shaking Scrooge's hand.

"I hope our next meeting won't be so tiring," said Launchpad. "I think I could sleep for a week!"

"Life is too short to waste it in bed!" Scrooge told him. "I can't wait to get back to my business."

When they landed at Duckburg Airport, Mrs. Beakley's niece, Webbigail, was waiting. As soon as Scrooge was off the plane, she gave him a big hug.

"I'm so happy to see you," she said. "I was afraid you'd come back younger."

"Why would that make you afraid?" asked Scrooge.

"Why? Because I like you just the way you are!"

DOUBLE-O-DUCK

The man in the raincoat glanced over his newspaper at Launchpad McQuack. "That's our man, XZ-34!" he whispered.

"He won't get away this time, XZ-35," came the reply.

When Launchpad was halfway between the two spies, they jumped on him and pinned him to the ground.

"Gotcha, Klaus Von Paten!"

"Let me go! My name's not Von Paten," said Launchpad.

They didn't listen. They dragged him to a warehouse, where a fierce-looking fat man held a bright light up to his face.

"Come on, Von Paten. Where's Dr. No's hideout?"

"I'm *not* Von Paten!" said Launchpad for the tenth time.

"Did you think you could fool us by dyeing your hair and changing your clothes?" asked the fat man. "I want the truth!"

"He's telling the truth, Boss," said a voice from the doorway.

Launchpad gasped. Handcuffed between two men stood someone who could have been his twin brother.

"Except for the hair, they're identical!" said Scrooge McDuck, who had come in by another door. "Who is he?"

"Klaus Von Paten, one of the most dangerous secret agents in the world. He works for the O.A.C.—the Organization of Associated Criminals. Dr. No is his boss."

Launchpad stood up. "Okay. Now that everything's cleared up, I'm leaving."

"Not so fast!" said the fat man. "The D.I.A. needs you."

"Of course it does," added Scrooge. "It's quite an honor. Few are called to such high service. Sign here."

"What is the D.I.A.?" said Launchpad.

"Duckland Intelligence Agency, our secret service," explained Scrooge. "Now, sign it, please. We haven't got all day."

Once Launchpad had signed the contract, they took him to a lab in the basement. He was surprised to find that Gyro Gearloose, the inventor, was also in on the secret mission.

"Gyro invents helpful gadgets for our agents," explained Scrooge. "Show Launchpad what you've made for him."

"Okay. If you're going to take Von Paten's place, you'll have to wear a black wig. I've hidden a pistol under it; to fire, you just pull the sideburns. There's also a tiny camera under your bow tie. But my best invention is this car!"

This was Gyro's masterpiece—a car that turned into a helicopter at the touch of a button!

Once the mission had been explained, and he had been disguised as Von Paten, Launchpad left for India. Stopping only for fuel and repairs, he soon landed in New Delhi.

Launchpad zigzagged through the city toward the Taj Mahal Cabaret. It was still early, but the place was full. Everyone wanted to see the famous dancer, Ducka Hari. Launchpad sat at a table at the edge of the dance floor.

"Four-zero-seven!" she whispered as she glided past.

"The new password?" he asked when she passed again.

"No, my room number. Be there in five minutes."

After a moment, Launchpad left his table and went to her room. When her dance ended, Dr. No's agent followed.

"Be with you in a minute, Darling," she promised, going into the next room.

She opened her bag and took out a comb, but it wasn't a comb. It was a telephone.

"Dr. No? I'm positive; Klaus Von Paten is either a double agent, or an imposter. What shall I do?"

Ducka Hari was beautiful. She was also a deadly expert in karate, and if Launchpad hadn't escaped quickly, his adventures as a secret agent would have ended then and there.

He raced to his car, but his enemy wasn't ready to let him go, and raced after him. Finally, Ducka Hari pushed him off the road and watched his car go over the cliff.

"What a pity," she sighed. "He was so good-looking."

She never thought for a moment that the false Von Paten would live through the accident. But, of course, Launchpad simply pushed the button that turned his car into a helicopter, and he never hit the ground.

In a few days, he was back on Ducka Hari's trail, watching her enter a grocery store in a Swiss village. After waiting an hour, he decided to go in after her.

Inside, she was nowhere to be seen. "She must be in the back," Launchpad thought. "How can I get in there?"

He left, and came back later carrying boxes of sausages.

"Sausage order," he said to the owner. "Shall I put it in back?"

"I didn't order sausages," said the shopkeeper. "There's been a mistake." But Launchpad had already gone through to the back of the shop, only to find that there was nobody there, either.

"Gee, it's cold in here," he said. "I'd better turn the temperature up or I'll freeze."

He touched the knob and right away a secret passage opened. Without a moment's hesitation, he entered.

The passage led to the underground lab, where Launchpad was surprised by Dr. No and his henchmen.

"Who are you working for?" demanded Dr. No.

"You can torture me, or even kill me, but I will never tell you that I'm with the D.I.A.!"

"You idiots! Did you think you could beat the O.A.C.? I'm going to rule the world, and nobody can stop me!"

Dr. No had his men throw Launchpad into the lions' pit with Ducka Hari. "I thought you were one of Dr. No's agents," he said to her.

"I'm here because of you. I told him you were dead, but you aren't."

"Let's talk about that later," said Launchpad, looking at the snarling lions. "Right now, I think those two are deciding which one of us to eat first."

He picked her up in his arms and clicked his heels together. Two springs hidden in his shoes sent them soaring to the top of the pit.

"That's some gadget," said Ducka Hari, impressed.

"We must call the D.I.A." said Launchpad. "May I borrow your comb?"

In no time at all, the D.I.A. forces were there to wipe out the O.A.C. once and for all.

Suddenly, the building was surrounded by special agents and commando forces.

"Dr. No is getting away!" cried Ducka Hari.

"You'll never get me!" growled Dr. No. He climbed out onto the lab's balcony and ran to the end. But there was no way out.

"It's the end of the road for you, Dr. No!" said Launchpad.

"No! Get out of my way!" Suddenly, the railing gave way.

"Take my hand!" yelled Launchpad. But it was too late. The evil Dr. No fell to the ground.

Launchpad was stunned. "Let's get out of here," he said. "It's all over."

"It's time to say good-bye," Launchpad said to Ducka Hari.
"Take me with you," Ducka Hari begged.
"It wouldn't work," said Launchpad. "I couldn't be a secret
agent in your world, and you would end up bored in mine."
And he turned and walked away to his helicopter.